THE RECOVERY OF HOPE

STORY OF A CIVIL CERVICES ASPIRANT

SHIVAM SINGH

Made with ♥ on the Notion Press Platform
www.notionpress.com

Dedicated

TO MY FAMILY

TO MY SOCIETY

TO MY COUNTRY

Contents

PREFACE

PREFACE
This is being written while my exams are being conducted. I have expressed his life directly on paper which is the story of a simple rural boy who fought with courage, faced difficulties and once again showed that a person can get victory on money and victory on failure by his burning desire and contineuous hard work. this story tells. that anone's past doesn't matter. as in this story a village boy who was neither a topper nor a Very bright student worked with all his effert to be an IAS officer and like other persons he also faces many problems in his way like deficiency of money, losing support of Parents and other distractions by mental feelings but he did not give up and kept working hard for achieving his goal and finally got it.. As it is being said by people that "A dream does not become reality through thoughts. or magic; it requires faith, determination. and hardwork"

Vijay just completed his graduation and is working with his father. His father is a poor man. altho Vijay is only son of his father but his father could not overcome Vijay's Desires. one night Vijay's father decided to let him study they took decision to send him To nearest city and prepare for civil services examination. Vijay agreed to this decision. Vijay an average student and was not very much bright. but he had desires to earn money and help his family's economy. Monday morning everything was arranged and it was time to let him go. "mamma did you put my charger in my bag ?" "Vijay I'm just doing it. Vijay you have to learn to do your things yourself, how often I will do this for you? " "just today mama" vijay laughed Vijay was happy to go city but he was also emotional because he was leaving his home and his mother. his father dropped him to bus stand with his old bike. as like other students Vijay was also given many responsibilities advises, blesses and the borrowed money which his father had borrowed from his teacher friend. Vijay was feeling responsible he was dedicated to his family and his goals. Vijay reached bus stand with many dreams thoughts and sorrow of leaving home. while sitting in bus his sad eyes saw his father and pearl like drops of tears fell down from his eyes. father journey and Vijay started a new journey towards city. new journey towards his dreams, towards a new World what he had never seen. everything was very new for him because he never went there. after a long journey of more than 2 hours the bus reached the city bus stand. everything was very new for him. Vijay was having a new experience he came out from bus and standing with his luggage called his village friend Amit who was 3 years elder and was preparing for civil services examination. "hello Amit hello Amit am Vijay yes yes I am here at the bus stand yes." (phone call disconnected.) Vijay was looking around his everything with surprising eyes because everything was new for him he looked around for 10 minutes and after that Amit came there with a bike along with his friend.Amit smile by looking Vijay and said him not to be tensioned about anything. "Amit I think this luggage is much and we cannot take it in bike. should we take a rickshaw?" asked Vijay "hmm I also think so. you are right we should take one." Amit called a rickshaw from road and said him to follow. Amit's friend went in rickshaw. and Vijay went with Amit on bike. Vijay saw such long high buildings of city he had never seen before he was very excited to see Amit's room and they reached there soon after journey of approximate 25 minutes. Amit room was on 2nd storey of the four storeyed building. they sat in room at most 5 minutes and rickshaw came there. both of them came down stairs to pull up the luggage up into the room. Vijay who had always seen open sky and breathed fresh air of village, feeling very uncomfortable there that small room and dim light was irritating him. bad smell of washroom could easily reach the room because bathroom was very near the room Vijay Vijay did not wanted to any minute there but there was no any option for him so he could not do anything he was looking around on the room and below the bed there was a study table everything was here and there nothing was arranged it didn't look like room of a student. Vijay thought he must be busy in studies so it is does not get time to do this all. "Vijay go and be fresh and then we will go for tea." said Amit Vijay didn't want to even the bathroom but there was no any other option for him so he had to use. "so is it done Vijay ?, let's go" said Amit "yes sure" both went for tea. at tea stall they discussed about a available room which amit's friend knew about. his friend told that one room is available at the third storey over his room. Vijay didn't had any much conversation skills so he didn't speak very much and just listened to others. he was learning to talk with urban people they came back to room and Amit friend Rahul asked for permission to leave and left the room. "Vijay We will seek for a room tomorrow because today I am feeling a bit tired and I need to sleep and you also should sleep." "I am also feeling tired Amit and I also think that I need to sleep and by the way it's 6:00 p.m. and it's time to sleep." NEXT MORNING they weaked up with alarm and Amit readed newspaper first. both talk about some topic and then after at least one hour they went Rahul's room to seek a room for Vijay. Rahul made a phone call to his apartment manager. "hello uncle Rahul speaking, yes yes actually that room Yes yes uncle on.. ok...ok" Rahul told that he is coming after sometime and they shall talk to him "Rahul how much you pay for your room ?" asked Vijay "I'm paying 5000 but it will be less for you because that room is big which I am using" "it's much Rahul my father even do not have profit of 5000 a month it's much for us maybe not for you"Said Vijay "but it's quite less than that of Delhi ,there is much rent taken by management, it's impossible to get a average room in 5000 there" till then room manager reached there and said "so let's come and first see it and if you like the room then we talk further" boys followed him and reached third storey man unlocked the door of room and said "come behind me hmm yes come this way see this is your kitchen how is it ? see how much space is here in the kitchen and come this side see this is your room and this window here you can keep a air cooler it's a big room say isn't it ?" "vijay say how is it ? , it's good for you vijay and also one best thing is this that Rahul lives here so he will also help you all the way" said Amit till now vijay kept quite he didn't say anything, they all came back to rahul's room and vijay agreed to live in the room this decision made amit most happy because he considered vijay as burden room costed 4100 per monthVijay said "uncle Aww Am Asking that when Should I pay the room rent?" "Vijay You can do so within next two three days and that Security fee I say pay me 5000 extra along with rent and that is your security fee, and you will have to Pay yourn next month's rent on 15th of every month" (At Amit's room) "Vijay should we go to buy other Households ? "But Amit Am thinking that i have to call my father and tell him about security fee because it's not very small amount am going to Pay" "Hello Hm Papa hm all is well hmm he is also well" "Papa I say. that house owner is demanding security fee along with rent" "ah Vijay tell me how much is it?" "Papa ... rent is founty one hundred and security 5000" "Vijay my Son you are there to study with all effort and if you need some more money i will arrange but first get settled there as soon as possible and start your studies and do not be tentioned, about money ok I will give you by arranging anyway, ok take Care" "Vijay should we now go otherwise we will come back at night because it will take at least 3-4 hours to buy all the needed things and bring to your room" AT STATIONARY SHOP "Vijay first decided which Subjects you are going to choose, are you Sure that you will select same as mine?" " am sure and if you have choosed it then i am sure that it must be good" Amit Showing folded piece of paper "this is list of books" and this way they buy books, furniture and other needed things for Vijay's new room. After 1½ hour... "It's All set up now." "Amit your today's dinner from my side at my new room" said Vijay "oh Vijay Bro Should I Invite my two friends from my side ? Umm actually one is my coaching friend and another is rahul " "Oh sure it will be my Pleasure" said vijay "So let's come to Rahul's room I show you his room and then I have to go" Vijay surprised to see Rahul's room it was quite different from Amit's also there was no any bad smell like Amit's room it looked like much clean and very managed Big World map sticked on wall and on the other side Pictures of Hollywood Actors and Actresses. Study desk below tube light and Much expansive music system at a corner. Suddenly Amit said "Hour much you will see Rahul's room vijay did you forget for what we came here?" "Oh yes. Rahul actually we are came here to invite you for today's dinner in my Room" Said vijay "Vijay Now let me go ok and we will meet at dinner and you start with NCERT books, first Read the books in which you are most interested and then increase it slowly" Vijay went in room and now he was alone in Room but his thoughts were not going to make him feel alone. the started with history book of class 8th and at once he continued four next three hours till then he felt that it was 6:05 PM and his doorbell was Buzzing. "One minute wait wait am coming" loudly said vijay Rahul, Ravi and Amit were there at the door with A Black Polythene hanging on the Amit's hand "Vijay, actually I know you are vegeterian and we have brought some Paneer four you and

Ravi and chicken for me and Rahul" "But i think we should not cook chicken in your room and so we will do dinner at Rahul's room." After some time....... "Rahul, How much is it?" said Amit "Chicken 500 and Paneer also 500 grams" said Ravi "first we will cook Paneer and then chicken" said Amit Afew minutes later .... "Ok finally it get prepared and now it's time to serve and enjoy" "Amit, should i now open the Bottle ? " said Rahul "Bottle! what which Bottle" said Amit "Amit come on don't try to be very innocent And by the way now Vyjay is also our group member how much we will keep it hidden. from him ? " said Rahul. "No No i am a group member but i do not drink" Said Vijay "you vijay i didn't intended that" said rahul "Vijay I am sorry i did not tell you that i learned to drink staying here but I don't drink very much, i take it occasionaly " said Amit "It's ok Amit " "And by the way it's culture of current generation" said Vijay at morning (Phone call) "Amit Hello Amit did you wake up or sleeping till now it's 7 AM Amit and what About Rahul and ravi are they also sleeping" said Vijay. Amit said "Hmm Vijay just get ready and we will go for your admission today" At the Raception of Sindhu IAS Builders "Come come this side yes " "most welcome to our coaching sindhu IAS" "Sire Please take your seat" said the lady. She further said "My Name Is Radhika. I am here to provide you admission So please tell me your name first." "Hii, this is vijay and I am Amit and am already studying here and Vijay wants to take admission" said Amit with a huge smile. "I know you and vijay, you just tell me your selected subjects and fill up this form" said reception lady "Ok ok subjects are same as Amit's and Iam filling it up" lady told him about fee and said him to pay the fee and get it done "take it it's my fees" Said vijay "give 500 extra kindly For form filling fee" Vijay said with surprising face "What 500 ?" "Yes sir, Sure" "ok Take this" said Vijay by handovering her a 500 "And "You will have to come at class time with Amit" "Ok ma'am thank you" "OK" Amit went to his room and Vijay went towards his one Vijay readed books till coaching time. and at 4:20 he made a Phone call to Amit "Hello, Amit coaching is at 4:30 AM i Right?" "Yes Yes you come now am and you will reach till 4:30" Replied Amit" Vijay went coaching and Amit also reached, both met at the door of coaching and went towards the class, "Vijay let's come and drink water before starting and sir will come after Some time" Vijay looked around every side of class room very carefully and he found many boys and girls sitting very seriously many close to each other some talking, some laughing, some arguing about any topic the whole Classroom was full of variations before it Vijay had always seen boys & girls sitting away from each other and talking to each other by distance but here things were different. Suddenly class's noise changed into silence, vijay saw every side and he found A 50 yeared man coming into class. "This is sandeep sir" said Amit "Good evening students" "Good evening sir" sounds of many students together "Hove Is it going on ? Is everything well?" "Yes Sir" again many students Replied. teacher started explaining and Vijay listened Carefully someone from back seat was disturbing him but he didn't say anything to him and concentrated in class After the class was over he came back to room & Everything gone well that day but he was not very happy because he missed this Mother and father Vijay was fnow a hardworking student and studied with all effort to get his family's dreams true at night while lying on bed he decided that will not waste his much time in talking about any useless topic and give his free time to extra current affairs topic and he felt in a deep sleep thinking that. with Morning alarm 5:30 AM vijay thinks (Oh how soon it became 5:30 but it is ok first i'll read newspaper and then daily routene after 3 hours he was feeling hungry and went to prepare tea And this way his second day and a week went well and Vijay learned many things, manners, way of talking during this week along with amit. It was friday and Amit was not came by some reason. And Vijay was first time without Amit in class to sat on a seat which was at Second row and a other boy also sat aside him. "Hello, I am Sumit Are you new in class?" said the boy "Yes I am Joining since last week" Vijay Replied "Oh so you are Regular from last week, by the way I was not here forom last 8-9 days so how could I See you" sumil said. Vijay forwarded his hand four handshake "friends?" "Sure, what's your name?" asked Sumit "my name?. Vijay". Class started and they both stopped talking. After class sumit left Vijay at Door of coaching and said "bye" Vijay started walking on road towards his way he was happy that day because he had made a friend and was thinking about sumit suddenly Someone called him from back "hey Vijay" Vijay turned his face back aud found a girl on Scooty coming towards him. Vijay was silent because he didn't believe that she called him beause vijay didn't even recognize that girl and looked surprisingly on her then the girl came hear and said "yes you see your bag you had left a book at class" Vijay opened his bag and got that his one book was missing from there he said "Oh yes am Sorry and thanks for it" girl passed a book to him "is this ?" "yes but how did you know my name and recognised me?" asked vijay "oh You man just don't ask this" girl left by saying "ok bye we will meet again" Vijay's mind totally changed by this incident till then he was thinking about sumit but Now He forgot him because his current mind was full from questions that who was that girl and she even didn't tell her hame and that how she knew my name also she helped me but why? that night Vijay tried to study but he could not concentrate he thought that she may be friend of any friends and made a Phone call to Amit and asked "Hey Amit did you tell any girl about me?" "No guy I did not do this". That night Vijay neither talked to his father or mother nor he studied much. he was so excited for next day and by the luck next day he sat aside the girl and Amit was sat away because vijay came first and then Amit. "hii I am vijay" "Yes I know that you are vijay tell me something different" said that girl vijay asked "What's your name?" "Radha" she replied. "And how do You knowe me?" again Vijay asked. "This is the thing i will never tell you and don't ask it again" she said And their conversation was stopped by a teacher's entry till next three days Vijay did not study even if he tried he could not once he opened book to Read and kept it opened and opened for hours and did not Read a sentence even. but after three days he found himself distracted from study he found his path loosing in Smoke and he waked up. decided to concentrate his mind on studies and Keep his limited attention towards Radha. at a evening Vijay's Phone ranged he picked the call of his father "hello vijay how are you my son? actually my Phone recharge was expired and you didn't call me since last 3-4 days then I rechanged my Phone and called you " "Am fine Papa actually I was a bit busy in studies that's why i couldn't contact you from four days , am Sorry for this" said vijay "It's ok boy carry on, keep Working hard you know vijay all society's eyes are looking. Just at you. and i hope you will do this soon........" and conversation continued. next day vijay didn't sit close to that Pretty girl he also didn't look towards her for first 15 - 16 minutes but then he could not controll himself and looked her she was also looking at him. and this way he again lost himself into the dark fog forgetting his own way to achieve his goals....... A Few Months Later till now vijay knows that the girl had got his information at a social media platform Midnight 11:49 PM "Radha we should work more because it's not enough for us and it's my first Attempt so i don't have any experience but you You can do it also you have done Prelims once so i hope you can do it" Said vijay Radha replied "See vijay I am trying my best but if you say I will study more from today. And i hope you will also do more studies from next day and we will talk less than 1 hour and give our most time to studies okay and for now just forget everything and fall into deep sleep okay bye good night" "bye Good night" said vijay (Phone call disconnected) Both were very loyal to their decision and started studies by next day and worked very hard to get passed in prelims and when result announced they got paid by their hard work , yes , both did it but it was not enough to do prelims only and that's why they both turned their phones off and started preparation of mains exam. after exam Vijay and Radha opened their phones and first Radha told her family that she did well in exam. Vijay was sad because he could not do well but when he know that radha did good examped merely and became happy his father also called him and asked about exams that Vijay asked for more time and his father agreed exactly for result and finally result announced this first day when coachings student over selected in mens and many students were saying in wine shops many weeping in front of their parents some warriors getting congratulations from everyone and Vijay and radha were mute this day Aldo Vijay was already eliminated but he was not sad that day as much as today.Ravi made a phone call to Vijay and told him that it's not over it's time to continue and prepare better for next time Radha called her parents and asked for one more chance but her father refused to give anymore. this time he said her to arrange money herself and by then arrangement of money became an issue for herbut she didn't give up also Vijay decided to share some part of his money with her but it didn't overcome her money requirements. and that's why she had to seek for a teaching job in a nearby coaching centre as a English teacher but her income was not much so see also had to borrow some money from her friends and she felt ashamed for it. Vijay always supported her but there were huge challenges in front of her in the biggest one was to save time because he teached in daytime so she had to complete her syllabus studies at night and this way she burn a fire mind and a desire to do it and worked very hard all the session. next year both went their respective residences to meet their families and Radha's father asked her about marriage because she was already 23 and her father said her that after this attempt she will not be allowed to live there and they will get her married. Vijay's father and mother also told him that they have sold their one acre of land and they will not give any more chance if he failed this time. both came back to city with many dreams and hopes and did better than last time exam day came and both of them were satisfied of their preparation and it was day to express their hardwork on answer sheet. Radha decided to pick Vijay with her scooty to examination centre but fortunately they faced an accident and both got injured her scooty was hitted by a car and was broken. due to serious injury they could not attempt exam and lost their hope. Vijay borrowed money from Sumit for his and Radha's treatment. it took more than one week to get them well and after all they didn't tell anything to their parents but now they had lost support of their parents and things became very hard for them but courage had made them

more strong. someone had said that "wound results in making of brave warriors" Vijay and Radha didn't give up they decided to try once more but problem was families permission Vijay's family could be made understand but what about Radha ? what should she do? is there any of other option for her? Vijay called his parents but they refuse to help him anymore , they said that he is already 28 yeared they also said him to go back , get married and start helping his father. both were very tension about their future two days passed Vijay and Radha could not do anything and could not decide anything they were in their respective rooms lying unhappily. Radha became hopeless but Vijay was still thinking about driving any way of getting one more chance. Midnight 1:13 AM Radha's phone ringing....
"Hello Radha were you asleep? Sorry to disturbence" said vijay "No vijay it's ok i was not sleepping tell what were you doing?" asked radha Vijay said "Radha I have an idea and this is only way to get continued" "What's that ?" "Radha we will leave one message to our Family explaining that we are going to continue and not need their support anymore and then we will take room at any other area and start t it with all our energy vijay explained. "But Vijay our families....."
"Radha this is the only way, try to understand. and we both will do some extra work for money arrangment and continue our preparation Both Vijay and Radha accepted this challange to Continue their preparation. and huge challanges become small after they are accepted and this way both lived together coperating each other and worked with all their energy till next exams and in this time period many people and their families tried to contact them but they could not reach because Vijay became Igniter and Radha made herself Fuel and the fire was in its long lasting mission........... After A Year Ravi is a middle class father who

lives with his wife and newly born daughter and cares his hardware shop. Rahul works in a private company along with his brother and now he doesn't drink "cold Bottle" Amit got chance as social science teacher and lives in a good well managed house. and sometimes talks to "Vijay sir " on phone call who is an IPS officer and lives in city with his PCS topper wife Radha ma'am........